Theseus
and the
Minotaur

by Laura North and Ross Collins

W
FRANKLIN WATTS
LONDON·SYDNEY

First published in 2009 by
Franklin Watts
338 Euston Road
London
NW1 3BH

Franklin Watts Australia
Level 17/207 Kent Street
Sydney
NSW 2000

Text © Laura North 2009
Illustrations © Ross Collins 2009

The right of Laura North to be identified as the author
and Ross Collins as illustrator of this Work has been asserted
in accordance with the Copyright, Designs and Patents Act, 1988.

A CIP catalogue record for this book is available
from the British Library.

ISBN 978 0 7496 8586 7 (hbk)
ISBN 978 0 7496 8590 4 (pbk)

Series Editor: Melanie Palmer
Series Advisor: Dr Barrie Wade
Series Designer: Peter Scoulding

Printed in China

Franklin Watts is a division of
Hachette Children's Books,
an Hachette UK company
www.hachette.co.uk

For Sue and Michael – L.N.

Long ago, Prince Theseus
lived with his father,
King Aegeus, in Athens.

One day, Aegeus told his son a terrible secret. "Every year we must send seven people to King Minos in Crete. He feeds them to the Minotaur, a terrifying monster."

Brave Theseus wanted to help. "Father, this time I will go with them and kill the beast!"

Theseus made his father a promise. If he lived, he would put a white sail on his ship. If he died, the sail would be black.

When Theseus arrived in Crete,
King Minos was waiting.
"Good, more food for the
Minotaur!" he laughed.

He sent the prisoners to the labyrinth, a huge underground maze where the Minotaur lived.

"I'll go first," Theseus cried.

"The beast doesn't scare me!"

As he was about to enter the maze,

a young woman stopped him.

"Wait," she whispered, "I'm
Ariadne, King Minos's daughter.
Let me help you." She had already
fallen in love with Theseus.

Ariadne gave Theseus a sword and a ball of thread. "These will help you kill the Minotaur and escape from the maze," she told him.

Theseus was so grateful that he promised to marry Ariadne if he lived. Then he tied the thread to the door and climbed down the steps.

For hours and hours he crawled in the darkness, leaving a trail of thread behind him.

Suddenly a huge shadow appeared.
Theseus saw a beast with the body
of a man and the head of a bull.

It was the dreaded Minotaur!

It had big yellow horns, blazing red eyes and teeth like daggers. It let out a blood-curdling roar, and ran straight at Theseus.

Theseus was too fast. He ducked away from the Minotaur's claws.

The beast was filled with rage.

As it charged towards him again,

Theseus pulled out his sword ...

... and plunged it straight into the Minotaur's chest.

It howled and dropped
to the floor. The Minotaur
was dead.

Theseus followed the thread out of the labyrinth. As he emerged, Ariadne was waiting for him.

Theseus took Ariadne to his ship and sailed back towards Athens. He couldn't wait to see his father.

But Theseus soon grew tired of Ariadne. One night, he left her asleep on an island and quickly sailed away.

In his rush to go home, Theseus forgot his promise. He had not changed the sail on his ship to white. It was still black.

Theseus was almost home when
Aegeus saw the black sail.
"My son must be dead!" he cried.
Full of grief, he leapt into the sea.

Theseus was heartbroken.

He named the sea the Aegean,

to always remember his father.

Puzzle 1

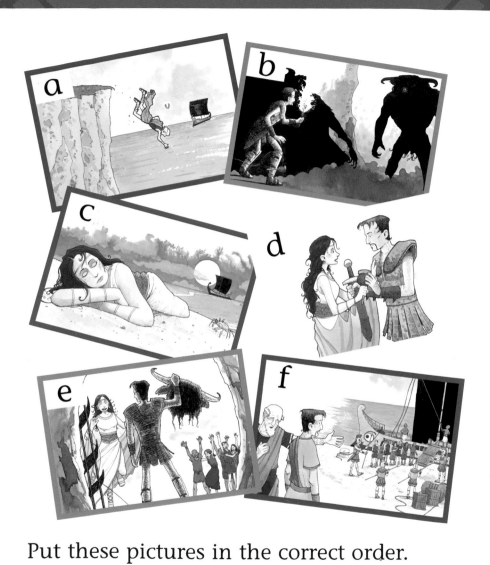

Put these pictures in the correct order.

Which event do you think is most important?

Now try writing the story in your own words!

Puzzle 2

Choose the correct speech bubbles for each character above. Can you think of any others? Turn over to find the answers.

Answers

Puzzle 1

The correct order is:

1f, 2d, 3b, 4e, 5c, 6a

Puzzle 2

Theseus: 2, 5

Ariadne: 3, 6

Aegeus: 1, 4

Look out for more Hopscotch Myths:

Icarus, the Boy Who Flew
ISBN 978 0 7496 7992 7*
ISBN 978 0 7496 8000 8

Perseus and the Snake Monster
ISBN 978 0 7496 7993 4*
ISBN 978 0 7496 8001 5

Odysseus and the Wooden Horse
ISBN 978 0 7496 7994 1*
ISBN 978 0 7496 8002 2

Persephone and the Pomegranate Seeds
ISBN 978 0 7496 7995 8*
ISBN 978 0 7496 8003 9

Romulus and Remus
ISBN 978 0 7496 7996 5*
ISBN 978 0 7496 8004 6

Thor's Hammer
ISBN 978 0 7496 7997 2*
ISBN 978 0 7496 8005 3

Gelert the Brave
ISBN 978 0 7496 7999 6*
ISBN 978 0 7496 8007 7

No Dinner for Anansi
ISBN 978 0 7496 8006 0

King Midas's Golden Touch
ISBN 978 0 7496 8585 0*
ISBN 978 0 7496 8589 8

Theseus and the Minotaur
ISBN 978 0 7496 8586 7*
ISBN 978 0 7496 8590 4

Jason's Quest for the Golden Fleece
ISBN 978 0 7496 8587 4*
ISBN 978 0 7496 8591 1

Heracles and the Terrible Tasks
ISBN 978 0 7496 8588 1*
ISBN 978 0 7496 8592 8

For more Hopscotch books go to: www.franklinwatts.co.uk

* hardback